Dragon Eggs Book 2

Dragon's Hope

Emily Martha Sorensen

Also by Emily Martha Sorensen

Books:

Black Magic Academy
The Keeper and the Rulership
The Fires of the Rulership
Worlds of Wonder
Tabby, Tabby, Burning Bright

Dragon Eggs:

Dragon's Egg

Fairy Senses:

Fairy Eyeglasses
Fairy Compass
Fairy Earmuffs
Fairy Barometer
Fairy Pox
Fairy Slippers
Fairy Lunchbox

Comics:

A Magical Roommate
To Prevent World Peace

http://www.emilymarthasorensen.com

For my friend Heather,
who always wants
more clean new adult fantasy.

And for my brother Michael,
who is constantly looking
for books about dragons.

CHAPTER 1
Hall

She wasn't really clear on why she was here, in the Hall of Saurischian Dragons, rather than getting ready for the day that was supposed to be the most important of her life. After all, she had a very full schedule today. Her roommates would be incredulous if they discovered where she'd snuck off to.

But something had drawn Rose back to the museum.

The crowd oozed past Rose as she watched the eleven *Deinonychus antirrhopus* dragon eggs that now remained in the display case. They lay there silently. Still.

"You're not dead," Rose murmured under her breath. "If Virgil wasn't, if another dragon out in Utah wasn't, you're all living, too. So wake up."

A cluster of children passed her, following a harassed-looking nanny. "Would you two stop poking each other?" the woman complained, separating a boy and girl who were jabbing fingers into each others' ears. "And you —!"

The milling mob of children passed in front of her, momentarily blocking the display case. As her view cleared, Rose held her breath, wondering if another egg had woken. But no. The mob was past. The nanny was gone.

Rose let out a long sigh.

She wasn't sure why it seemed so important to her that the other eggs awakened. She certainly was not looking to adopt a second child; she barely knew what she and Henry would do with the first one. Why was it that it mattered to her, then?

Rose stood there, lost in thought, troubled by the fervency of her desire. What was it? What was the reason?

The eggs did nothing. The crowd kept passing in front of her, sometimes jostling her, sometimes blocking her view, but always the eggs remained the same, still and in deep hibernation. Hibernation, because surely they must still be alive.

Why? Why did it matter so much?

Of course there was the obvious answer. As a prospective paleontologist, she had every reason to be fascinated by the prospect of living dragons. The fact that one had chosen her to be his mother bore no weight: she could not treat her son as a research subject. She, in fact, dared not. Another person's dragon child, however, she could treat with scientific objectivity. She would dearly like to have such an opportunity.

Then, too, there was the fact that Virgil was currently the only living dragon in this part of the country. Were he to be the only member of his species within his lifetime, it would be difficult to play with other children safely, or to feel like he had any place in the world other than as a relic, a living fossil of an ancient and long-dead age.

No child deserved to feel that way.

A raucous little boy burst out laughing as he ran toward the *Tyrannosaurus rex* skeleton displayed prominently behind her. "Its wings are tiny!" he shouted. "Its arms are even smaller! It looks so dumb! Ha ha ha!"

Rose closed her eyes. Mockery of a skeleton was one thing. But would her son have to deal with similar thoughtlessness from other human children his age?

Please hatch, Rose thought, blinking back tears. *Not for my son's sake. I'm more selfish than that. I don't want to be the only mother to a dragon in New York City. I don't want to be the only one going through this.*

Chapter 1: Hall

Oh, there was Henry, of course. But Henry's cheerful optimism and unflagging enthusiasm seemed to belie any real understanding of the challenges they were going to have to face. When Rose attempted to speak to him of all her worries, he simply turned a deaf ear, or else changed the subject to something more positive.

Perhaps he did it because he saw no value in borrowing trouble that might never surface. Perhaps he preferred to focus on the prospect of fatherhood, in which he seemed to take unending delight. That was valid. But to Rose, who felt far more terror than joy at the prospect of parenthood, it was also isolating.

If another dragon hatched, she thought, *there would be another woman in the city who would understand how I feel. Perhaps it wouldn't even matter who she was.*

All the professors and paleontologists and zoologists who had quietly and confidentially assembled to study the dragon were men. Rose wanted their respect, not their dismissal, so she dared not speak to any of them about feelings. One day, after all, she hoped to be among them, and to act like an emotional woman in front of them would only sabotage this.

Please hatch, Rose thought to the eggs, knowing that they could understand her meaning without her speaking aloud. *Please wake up. Please choose parents. I don't want to be alone in this.*

The eggs did nothing. Well, perhaps she couldn't really blame them. They were fetuses. They couldn't be expected to understand an adult's concerns, even if any of them were on the verge of waking.

Rose swallowed her emotions, as she had grown used to doing, and tried to leave. Then she turned back and spoke aloud.

"If not for me, then for yourselves," she said. "Perhaps you do not understand this. Perhaps it is ridiculous to even say it to you. But I will say it, nonetheless. You are not mere refugees from the past: you are the future of *Deinonychus antirrhopus,* a future that can only exist if your species becomes viable. The more individuals who hatch, the better that chance."

The eggs did nothing. Rose spoke again, this time forcefully.

"I do not know what mechanism you've used to hibernate. Whatever it is, it is extraordinary, to have preserved you so long and so well. It defies our current understanding or capacity for explanation. But one thing is clear: as long as you were all asleep, it was in your best interests to remain that way together. But now that even one has wakened, it is in your best interests to follow, so that you may be of compatible ages. Perhaps you are too young to consider your own offspring, but nature is not so merciful that you can ignore it. You *must* hatch now, if you want your species to have the best chance to survive."

The eggs did nothing. She had not really expected them to. Important as her words were, it was too much to expect not-even-infants to understand them.

Rose sighed heavily and turned away from the display case. A little girl with a sticky face was sucking on her fingers and watching her, and a whole family was staring at her oddly. Embarrassed, realizing she probably should not have said so much aloud before any announcement had been made, Rose walked briskly away towards the stairs.

She had spent far too long at the American Museum of Natural History today already. Her roommates would wonder where she had been.

Ducking through the crowd, not stopping to walk through the Hall of Ornithischian Dragons despite the fact that it had been weeks since she'd been there, Rose headed down the stairs, out the entrance, and into the street. Breathing in the odoriferous air, she settled into the walk through Central Park to reach her apartment.

It was a lovely Saturday morning, half-past ten, and there were families and nannies all over the park.

Will this be Henry and me in a few weeks? Rose wondered. *Or will we be too much celebrities once our son hatches and the newspapers are given the story?*

They hadn't even told their families about the dragon yet. She and Henry had discussed it at length, and he had said he didn't think his brother could keep a secret, while she had expressed concern about her nosy sisters and their love of gossip.

It wouldn't be long before they knew now, though.

Rose checked her wristwatch, and then picked up her skirts to walk more quickly. She had definitely stayed at the museum much longer than she should have. She didn't want to be late to her wedding.

CHAPTER 2
Here

"Where were you?" Henry demanded as she bustled past him into her parents' house, closely followed by her roommates, who had griped most of the trip that she hadn't left them any time to do her hair up nicely.

"Delayed," Rose said perfunctorily. She didn't want to explain where she had been, lest it exasperate him. There wasn't time to speak with him privately about dragons, anyway. "I lost track of time. I'm here now."

"Rose!" her mother cried, rushing in from the living room. "Where have you been? We've only half an hour before the minister arrives!"

"And my sister-in-law isn't getting along very well with your father," Henry added.

Rose felt weary.

"We tried to get here in time, but she didn't come back until half past ten," Natalie said in her usual bossy tone. "She said she'd been off on a walk. I think she was trying to run away."

"Natalie!" Penelope hissed, scandalized.

Henry caught Rose's eye, glancing over at her roommates as if to ask whether there were any truth to this. She shook her head in irritation. He looked relieved.

"Upstairs!" Rose's mother ordered, making shooing motions. "We need to get you ready!"

Rose gladly obeyed, mounting the stairs with haste. Her mother followed swiftly at her heels.

The dress was laid out on her bed, waiting for her. Rose suppressed a sigh. It wasn't really one she would have chosen for herself. It was lovely, with a scoop neckline and an elegant train, but it didn't feel like her. It was too soft, too gentle, too womanly. Her mother had worn it twenty-two years ago, and it had suited her mother perfectly. Had Rose chosen her own, she would have gone with something much more simple and plain.

But practicality was practicality. There had been no time to have her own dress made, nor would there have been the money. Rose's father had chosen to show his intense dislike of the groom by tightening his purse-strings.

Fair enough. It was sufficient that he had consented at all. At first, he had seemed likely to refuse outright, but then Rose's mother had taken him aside and spoken with him, and he had come back with a surly expression and an agreement that a wedding could be held in their home, but there would be no money paid for non-necessities.

Rose didn't know what her mother had said, but she had a nasty feeling that her parents, and most likely all of her and Henry's relations, were assuming she was pregnant. What other conclusion could they come to, when the two of them had announced the engagement so suddenly and insisted that the wedding be only two weeks away?

In fact, that conclusion wasn't far from the truth. There *was* a child on the way, a child that made their marriage the most sensible thing.

Still, it rankled to think that such assumptions might be spreading, even if they could be corrected later. Rose strongly suspected that her roommates had spread rumors about her to all their acquaintances.

"You look lovely," Rose's mother said, buttoning the dress up the back. There were dozens of tiny buttons.

Rose held her tongue and did not complain, though the dress was slightly too tight at the waist and squeezed her ribcage. "Thank you, Mama," she said politely.

"We'd best do something with your hair, too," her mother said, fingers moving busily.

Rose stood still, watching her reflection in the mirror as her mother bustled about. *Poor Mama,* she thought. *It must be such a disappointment to her that this is all the wedding she'll get from me. I suppose Sara and Louise will have to make up for it in lavishness, when their turns come in a few years.*

They were soon heading downstairs, and the next hour passed in a surreal blur. It was a ceremony just like any she had attended for cousins or her mother's acquaintances, only this time it was her standing before the minister, speaking the traditional words, and accepting the kiss from the young man who, in other circumstances, might have been a favorite beau, but instead was little more than a stranger. As family members rose from their chairs to share congratulations, Rose felt a curious sense of unreality.

This is it, then, she thought. *It's official.*

She wondered how Virgil was doing. When they had left him last night, he had been complaining about feeling tight within the egg, which meant he must be close to hatching. How much longer would they have? One week? Two?

Rose's mind raced as she thought about the preparations they had made. Every person had had different theories about what a *Deinonychus antirrhopus* infant might eat, or what might be the closest equivalent they could concoct. There were now four leading theories, and one of Rose's prevailing worries was that none of them would be adequate.

Of course all of them had asked Virgil, but his responses had been confusing and less than optimally helpful. It seemed clear he didn't understand what they were asking, and perhaps he didn't even have enough relevant memories from his parents to share in the first place. And of course, all of the prey species his parents had devoured were now extinct.

Mr. Teedle had immediately sent a telegram to the Dragon National Monument to inquire what they had fed their dragon hatchling, upon reading the news that one had hatched there, but there had not yet been a reply.

Rose rather suspected that he had failed to communicate any sense of urgency, and thus it had been buried in a pile of other inquiries from curious scientists and eager journalists.

Thus it was that there were now stockpiles of rats, frogs, insects, pigeons, and chickens filling an icebox that had been lugged into the laboratory where Virgil was currently settled. Every day, one of the professors brought a new bag of ice to keep the potentially-needed ingredients fresh.

Rose quailed at the thought of all the effort that was being put into the preparations to keep their son alive. Quite honestly, she would have preferred to leave him to the care of the dozen capable specialists for several more weeks. But no: the deal was that as soon as they were married, they were to take the egg home so that the empty laboratory could be used for scheduled classes again.

Presumably this meant that the whole icebox would be moved to their apartment, and that the researchers would continue visiting their home on the same constant schedule that they currently maintained in the laboratory they were borrowing.

And she was less than thrilled that the apartment Henry had rented for them was within an easy walking distance of City College, but over an hour's walk from Hunter College. He hadn't even asked her opinion before he'd taken it.

I'll have a long walk to school on Monday, Rose thought, feeling sick. Her roommates had already found another student at their college to replace her, and one of her professors had made an offhanded comment that implied he thought she would drop out of school before the semester was finished. It was as if nobody thought her education mattered.

"Congratulations," Henry's grandfather told Rose stiffly, shaking her hand. He seemed like a very formal gentleman.

"Thank you," Rose said politely, snapping back to the moment. This was her first introduction to most of Henry's family members. She should really make an effort to pay attention to them.

Then she looked over at Henry, and realized with a start that Mr. Teedle was standing next to him.

What? Rose thought, startled. *Did we invite him?*

She barely had time to wonder before the man opened his mouth and blurted out words that were both quick and rather too loud.

"The egg is hatching! You need to come right away!"

CHAPTER 3
Hurry

Outside the door, a cab was waiting. They rushed out to meet it, heedless of their family and neighbors shouting out and murmuring after them.

"Where do you think you're going?" Rose's father thundered, with an air of extreme offense.

Rose didn't stop to answer. It would only provoke an argument, which would delay their exit longer. She was not going to miss the hatching.

"Henry?" an elegant woman with an arrangement of curls called. She had been introduced as his mother. "Henry!"

He made no move to stop, either. The two of them scrambled up into the cab, Mr. Teedle following after them. Scrunched in between the two men, Rose wound her train around her arm in hopes that it would not not get caught in the enormous wheels on the way.

"Where are you going?" Rose's mother shouted as the the cabbie flicked his reins and the horses began moving forward. "Rose! *What egg?*"

The cab jostled around them as they drove down the city streets. There was a tense silence as they waited to arrive.

"I take it you haven't told your families?" Mr. Teedle asked.

"My mother is a gossip," Henry said briefly.

"So are my sisters," Rose added.

Mr. Teedle nodded silently.

"I think we should tell them before any announcements in the papers, mind you," Henry put in.

"Oh, well, obviously," Mr. Teedle agreed.

Rose wound the train around her arm more tightly, wondering when that would be. When she thought of telling her parents, of introducing them to the egg . . . no, soon to be the hatchling . . . her mind rebelled to even imagine it. How would her father react to the news that there were dragons alive? What about her mother and sisters?

She had only just made Henry's family's acquaintance. They lived just far enough out of the city to make traveling inconvenient, so she had only met them today.

They would be even more of a mystery.

When they reached the City College campus, Mr. Teedle directed the driver down the streets until they reached the appropriate building. Mr. Teedle was quick to dismount. He offered Rose his arm to help her get down, and then went to pay the cabbie as Henry hopped out. Henry made no move to wait. He strode straight up the stairs towards the entrance.

"Mr. Teedle," Rose said anxiously, "do you mind if I . . .?"

"Go ahead," Mr. Teedle said, waving his arm.

Rose hurried up the stairs after Henry, with some difficulty because of her dress. Henry held the door for her at the top, and she followed him in.

"Five dollars!" Mr. Teedle expostulated behind them. "That can't have been more than five miles! You must be joking!"

They ran down the hallway, Rose's heels clacking loudly against the floor. Unlike most days, when they had to dodge students, the building was empty.

It's rather nice not to receive odd looks for being here, Rose thought briefly. Since the school was for men only, she had had to pretend to be looking for Henry if anyone asked. One of his roommates had stopped her once, to chide her for going into a building where "women had no business being."

As if women can't study sciences, too! Rose thought, remembering the indignation she had felt that day.

They reached the door to the laboratory that was not currently being used for classes. The window was blocked so that no curious onlookers could peer inside, and Henry patted his pockets for the key. He stared at Rose in distress.

"I didn't bring mine, either," she said. "Knock."

Henry knocked on the door. "This is Henry Wainscott," he called. "Rose Palmer is with me. Would you please let us in?"

There was rustling, then footsteps, and the door opened. There were six men inside, all scientists that Rose recognized.

"Are we too late?" she asked breathlessly, rushing inside as the man held the door for her. Henry followed after her. "How is Virgil?"

"See for yourself," another of the men said, drawing aside. The egg was on the floor, nestled within a nest of blankets. Off to the side was the teddy bear Henry had bought for their son, a ridiculous gesture that Rose had objected to.

At first, the egg seemed the same as always. But then she noticed there were tiny cracks at the edges. She walked around, and saw that the cracks were much larger on the side that hadn't been facing them.

"Is he all right?" she asked anxiously. "He's not saying anything."

"He has been," one of the professors said. "It's just —"

The egg jostled, a noticeable jump. He was very, very upset that nobody was helping him!

"That," the professor said. "That's what he's saying."

Henry started to move forward. One of the men, a zoologist, put out his hand to block him.

"No," the man said. "The dragon's shared no memories of any ancestors being helped with hatching. I don't think he's supposed to be helped."

"But —" Henry protested.

"If you help a chick hatch out of an egg, it'll die," the man said firmly. "We don't know if that's true for dragons, but it wouldn't be wise to risk it. He must do this himself."

Another crack spread across the egg. It jostled. He was very, very, very upset!

Henry let out a small moan.

Rose unwound the train from her arm, anxious to do something. She had been horrified to think of him hatching without her, but now it was unbearable to stand here waiting.

The egg jostled again. No new cracks spread across it.

Virgil was miserable. He was very, very miserable. He was stuck and he was miserable and he just wanted to sleep. Nobody was helping. He was very unhappy.

"How long will it take?" Henry asked pitifully.

"There were cracks on that side of the egg when I came," one of the men said. "That was two hours ago."

"My wife took more than eight hours to deliver our son," another man said.

Rose shuddered. That wasn't something she wanted to think about.

There was nothing from the dragon for a long time. Rose wondered whether he really had gone to sleep. Was that normal for a dragon? She didn't think it was normal for most other creatures. She was just about to ask when the egg wriggled vigorously.

He was stuck and he was uncomfortable and he was STUCK STUCK STUCK! He wanted to get out, he wanted to get out, he wanted to get OUT! *OUT, OUT, OUT!*

"You can do it," Henry gasped, clenching his fists. "You can do it. Please!"

The door rattled behind them, and Rose spun around to glance back. Mr. Teedle shut the door behind himself and put away his key. "Five dollars, indeed," he was muttering.

"Ooh!" one of the men shouted. "That's another crack!"

Furious with herself for getting distracted, Rose spun back. The crack was stretching further . . . further . . . further . . .

"He's going to do it," Henry gasped. "He's going to do it!"

"Let me see!" Mr. Teedle said, elbowing one of the other men off to the side so that he could get through them.

Virgil was scrunched and stuck and miserable and he was VERY, VERY, VERY UPSET!

There was a cracking sound, and something tiny and sharp poked through the center of the fractured web.

"It's an egg tooth!" the man standing next to Rose shouted.

Everyone rushed to their side of the egg. Rose was so crowded in among them that she could scarcely breathe, but she didn't care. Almost as one, they all held their breath.

"Is he green?" Henry murmured.

"Were *Deinonychus antirrhopus* dragons green?" another man wondered.

"We have no way of knowing," Mr. Teedle said reverently. "This is our first time finding out."

It's not true that we have no way of knowing, Rose thought. He's shared some of his parents' memories, including how they saw each other. His father was blue, and his mother was green . . .

A whole snout burst through, and there were shouts and cheers around them.

Virgil was angry! Why were they making noise instead of helping him? They were right there!

"You're almost out," Henry said eagerly. "You're almost out, Virgil. Come on! You can finish! I know you can!"

A huge section of egg broke free and shattered across the floor. Behind it they could see a glimpse of a tiny face, and a tiny claw gripped the edge of the opening.

The dragon's head shot out, dripping and shiny, with tiny nubs where horns would soon be. The egg toppled forward, and his head smacked the floor. Virgil struggled further, and another claw emerged from the egg. Then another. Then a whole arm. Then a leg.

At last, only the tail was still left within the egg. It tapered down into a wet and sticky mess behind him.

Virgil was mad. Virgil was very tired.

Virgil was hungry.

CHAPTER 4
Hungry

"Food," one of the professors said out loud. "We have to feed him. What are we going to start with?"

"I want to be the first to feed him," Henry said immediately. "Unless . . ." He looked over at Rose, his expression guilty. "Do you want to be first?"

"No," Rose said. Quite honestly, she didn't even want to be the second. "You can be first."

"Do we have anything prepared?" Mr. Teedle demanded, looking around at one of the other men.

One of the other professors cursed, with rather shocking language. "I'm sorry. I meant to get something started, once the egg was hatching . . . but in all the excitement . . ."

"Do we have anything even *thawed?*" Mr. Teedle demanded.

"Rheinhold was going to do that, and he's not here," a professor said uncomfortably.

Are they really going to waste time assigning blame? Rose thought incredulously. "Then start with insects," she said briskly she said briskly to the biology professor who stood near her. "Pull them out and cook them over a Bunsen burner until they're thawed. Then cool them down however necessary, so they won't burn his mouth. And you," she added, turning to the man next nearest her, "you do the same with the meats."

16

The men nodded and hurried to the icebox. Two other men started to set up Bunsen burners.

"What else do we need?" Henry asked. "Do we have a . . . prepared recipe?"

"We'll have to develop that as we see what he accepts and rejects," Mr. Teedle said.

Rose said nothing. She knew what they were all thinking. *If he rejects everything, if the only things he could eat went extinct millions of years ago, he'll starve to death. We'll have no way to save him.*

Surely that wasn't going to happen, though. Surely their son would be all right. Surely the baby would eat.

Please eat, Rose thought. *Please don't put us through what Mama went through with her daughters. We can't hire a wet nurse, like she had to. Please eat.*

Virgil was sleeping on the floor. Rose crept closer to watch him. His chest moved in and out as he breathed, and his tail twitched in the slime of the egg. She wanted to move forward, to clean him off, but she wasn't sure if that would wake him. She didn't want to wake him, not before they had food ready.

Please eat, Rose prayed. *Please . . . be able to eat what we have prepared.*

Three men were clustered around each of the Bunsen burners.

"Don't cook the crickets too much," one of the men opined. "They must have eaten raw food."

"How do you know?" another man challenged. "They breathed fire. One of the prevailing theories is that most dragons cooked their food."

"Cook some of the crickets and leave the rest as raw as you can," Mr. Teedle said, moving over to them. "It's very likely that adult dragons preferred roasted food, or at least didn't mind it. They presumably used their fire for hunting. But we don't know about infants."

"Cooking meat makes it more digestible," another man said. He was holding a frozen chicken while another man set up a tripod to put it on. "That's why we do it."

"So cook most of the chicken," Mr. Teedle said. "We'll try it with various pieces at varying levels and see what he'll accept. What about the rats? Who's thawing a rat?"

"I'm going to do it just as soon as I'm done with these insects," one of the men over a Bunsen burner grunted, stirring something in a small bowl that was set over the tripod. "Yes, I think these are close to thawed. Here, you," he said, turning off the Bunsen burner and picking up the bowl gingerly in his gloved hands. He set it on the table on a mat that had been laid out for it. "Crush these into a paste. We can be reasonably certain that the babies didn't eat their food whole."

Henry nodded and picked up a pestle.

The door rattled, and two men rushed in. They were both paleontologists who worked with Mr. Teedle.

"Did we miss it?" one of them asked.

"Traffic was horrible on Broadway," the other one added.

"He's over there," Mr. Teedle said in a low voice. "He's sleeping."

The two men looked crushed, but then they crept over to that part of the room, and one of their faces lit up. The other just looked fascinated.

I know, Rose thought, smiling slightly. *I know.*

"Can we touch him?" one of them asked.

Henry's head shot up.

"We don't know yet," Rose said. "Better not to risk it. We'll wait until Henry feeds him."

"Do you think he might catch a chill?" one of the men asked. "Maybe we should put a blanket on him."

"He might be temperature insensitive," the other one said. "Dragons breathed fire, after all."

"It's doubtful that the infants did," the first one objected. "We don't want him to get ill."

"The egg didn't need incubation," Rose spoke up. "Not in the past few weeks, and not in his parents' memories. The mechanism that produced fire must at least be sufficiently active to keep him warm."

The men fell silent, and all three of them watched the dragon.

The mechanism that produced fire, Rose thought. Her veins tingled in excitement. Dragon fire was one of the great mysteries in paleontology. Where it had come from, what had produced it, and what the many dragon species had used it for . . . those were all subjects of intense debate.

One of her goals had long been to be the paleontologist who discovered the answers to those mysteries. And now, perhaps, the answer to all of those questions was lying in front of them, sleeping.

It was both exciting and frustrating. Exciting, because she could hardly wait to find out all the things Virgil would teach them about his species. Frustrating, because she had promised herself not to think of him as a subject of research. How would she do that? How could she possibly reconcile her curiosity with the fact that he needed a mother who looked at him lovingly, not clinically?

Rose glanced over at Henry, who was grinding crickets without complaint.

If I fail, at least he'll have Henry to be affectionate, she thought. *The man was almost built to be a parent.*

But with that thought came some jealousy. Why did it come so easily to Henry? What did he have that she was lacking?

"Should I pour some water in this?" Henry asked. "Presumably he'll have to get water from someplace."

"Yes, tentatively, but let's try it without first," the man next to him said. "I really should have thought to remove the hair from this rat before we froze it," he added.

Henry wrinkled his nose. "I hope rats aren't the thing he likes best. I don't favor the idea of capturing them."

"I don't think you *should* capture them, even if he does favor them," the man said. "Rats often carry disease, and they're often poisoned. You don't want that being ingested by the dragon."

Rose shuddered at the idea.

"So we'd have to buy them?" Henry asked. "Presumably from the same people who supply them to laboratories?"

"That would be my recommendation," the professor said.

"Wouldn't insects have the same potential problems?" Rose spoke up. "Presumably pigeons, as well?"

"Oh, yes," Mr. Teedle said. "Better to only stick with food you can buy."

Henry looked even less thrilled.

Rose sighed. He had refused to show her his finances, but she assumed he was worried about the expense. No wonder, since his budget would now have to stretch to feed three.

He had insisted that the money wouldn't be a problem, and that she didn't have to worry about it. He'd claimed the stipend from his grandfather would be sufficient for whatever they needed. But she wondered. Full-grown *Deinonychus antirrhopus* dragons were twice the size of humans, and the speed at which they grew to adulthood was still a mystery.

Please eat, she thought to Virgil. *And please don't eat so much that we can't afford it.*

The tiny dragon stirred, and his eyes opened. His tail flicked one of the eggshell fragments, which skittered across the floor. Everyone in the room stopped what they were doing, fixated on the sight of the small dragon.

Virgil was hungry. He wanted his parents to feed him.

CHAPTER 5
Health

"rickets first?" Henry asked, looking very nervous.

"Crickets first," Mr. Teedle confirmed.

Henry moved forward, carrying the bowl with him. He held it in his bare hands, which implied that it had cooled enough to be handled comfortably. Hopefully that meant the contents were also sufficiently cooled . . . if that even mattered in the case of dragon infants.

Henry's arms shook as he sat down on the floor beside the tiny dragon. "Hello, Virgil," he said. "I'm your father. Do you remember me?"

Virgil recognized his father's mind, but his father looked strange. Where were his horns and claws?

"I don't have horns and claws," Henry said. "I've tried to explain this to you before. We're human. We're a different species."

Virgil didn't understand. Virgil was hungry.

"Okay," Henry said. He swallowed several times, visibly. "I have some food for you here. Try this."

He reached into the bowl and pulled out a mashed-up bug. He held it out.

The tiny green-scaled dragon just stared at it. He felt very reproachful. That wasn't food. His father should know what food was. Why was his father giving him something not-food?

"All right," Henry said. His voice was steady, but his hands were shaking. "Would you please explain what food is?"

Food was food! His father was supposed to feed it to him! He should open his mouth, and then Virgil would eat from it!

"You want me to . . . uh . . ." Henry stared down at the bowl. "No, I'm not going to put crickets in my mouth. Sorry."

Virgil didn't want that not-food! Virgil wanted *food!* His parents should give him food! Virgil was getting very, very upset!

"What do I do?" Henry asked the rest of them, looking panicked.

Let me try, Rose thought, but she didn't say it. If she failed at this . . . if she failed . . . she wasn't used to failing, and the thought of failing when a child's life depended on their success terrified her.

"Let me try," one of the men said. "I've nursed a baby pigeon back to health once. My wife has a soft spot for them."

Looking angry, and embarrassed, and relieved, and unsure of himself, Henry hesitated and then handed the bowl over. The man took them and knelt down by the hatchling.

"There's nothing to be afraid of," he said coaxingly. "Just try this little bit. If you don't like it, we can try something else. We just have to see if this will work."

Virgil opened his mouth and let out a high-pitched, piercing shriek.

Rose reflexively covered her ears as the high pitch grew louder and louder. She saw most of the men in the room had done the same thing.

Virgil was very, very angry and offended! He would tell them that while he was breathing! Now he would scream again!

"No, please don't —" Rose began.

The unbearably high pitched scream started up again.

"Virgil," Henry said in distress, moving closer to the dragon. He put his hand on the nubs where his horns would be. "Virgil. It's all right. If you want me to feed you, I'll feed you."

The shriek stopped.

Virgil was sad. Virgil was angry. Not-parents couldn't give him food! Only parents could give him food!

"All right," Henry said anxiously. "All right. I'll even put it in my mouth if you want."

He took the bowl from the man who held it and plunged his fingers in, then hesitated for a long moment, his fingers hovering over the mashed crickets. He looked like he was trying to force himself to move.

No! Virgil didn't want that! That wasn't food! Virgil wanted the food his mother and father had already made for him! In their mouths!

"Uhhhhh . . ." Henry said. "What?"

In their mouths! In their mouths, in their mouths, in their mouths! Virgil was hungry! Virgil was getting upset again!

"Oh, no!" a man across the room cried. His face had gone pale. "Crop milk! He's talking about crop milk. I don't know how we're going to replicate that!"

"Crop . . . what?" Henry asked. His arms were tight with tension. "What are you talking about? Dragons aren't mammals!"

"Neither are birds, and crop milk is a way some birds feed their young," the man explained. "I can't believe it never even occurred to us that . . ."

"It occurred to me," Mr. Teedle said, running his hand through his well-oiled hair in agitation, "but I didn't think it would actually be a concern. There's a theory that dragons were the evolutionary ancestors of birds, but I've never put much stock in it, as the wyverns like *Pterodactylus antiquus* would make much more sense as ancestors, being four-limbed just like birds are, whereas dragons are six-limbed, unlike any other living creature in the world today —"

"Excuse me," Henry broke in, his face turning red with anger. "Can we get back to my son? How do we feed him if we can't replicate the equivalent of mother's milk for him?"

Virgil was getting very hungry. Virgil was getting very tired. Maybe he would scream again.

Two men's hands flew to their ears.

"We feed him what we can," Rose said firmly. She walked past the two men standing beside her, knotted the train of her dress around her waist, and knelt down on the floor by Virgil. Perhaps this would make her dress filthy, though she hoped she could avoid that, but right now, the baby mattered far more.

"Virgil," she said, "we don't have what you're asking for. I'm sorry. We'll have to try whatever we can. It might make you sick. But it's far better than not trying."

Virgil was confused. They'd agreed to be his parents. They should have started to make food then. Why hadn't they made him food? Didn't they love him?

Beside her, Rose saw Henry's fists clench.

The little dragon's tail twitched. He was starting to look lethargic. His eyelids drooped, and he let out a pitiful memory of hunger.

"Henry," Rose said, "open your hand."

"But he won't take —" Henry began.

Rose seized Henry's hand, scooped up a small handful of cricket mash, and slapped it in his palm. Then she put his other hand on top, connected at the wrists and open in front.

"Virgil," she said, "there's a mouth here. Eat the food in it."

Virgil's eyelids drooped. He raised his head and pushed at the hands with his nose. His snout somehow found his way into them. His tongue snaked out and licked the cricket mash.

Virgil's eyes flew open, and he jerked back. He let out a long, high-pitched scream.

Hands flew up to cover ears all over the room.

Virgil's mother had betrayed him! Virgil's mother had lied to him! That wasn't a mouth! That wasn't food! That was something! That was not-food! That was *something!*

"Yes," Rose said sternly, her hands in her lap. She made no move to cover her ears. "That was *something.* Something that might possibly work as food."

That was not-food! That was something! That was not-food! Virgil was very upset!

Henry bit his lip. He looked on the verge of tears.

"Yes, it was very unfortunate," Rose said coldly. "But it might also keep you alive."

Virgil was very upset! Virgil was very upset! Virgil was very, very, very *UPSET!*

Rose said nothing. If she let herself feel bad for him, she wouldn't have the firmness of will to force him to eat until they found something that he would partake of willingly.

"Perhaps it would help to buy lemon juice, and use that as a marinade," one of the professors said into the silence. "That can help break meat down. Make it easier to digest. He might need something like that, since presumably he's not supposed to be eating solid foods yet."

"Good idea," Mr. Teedle said. "We might also ask a butcher to save us intact stomachs. The juices in there might be helpful to break down food."

There seemed to be no question that they were all staying. Though Mr. Teedle did order one of the men to go to a butcher and buy cow, pig, lamb, turkey, and any other meat available that they did not already have on hand, as well as any intact stomachs that might be available.

"A whole bird, such as a chicken or turkey, if necessary," Mr. Teedle added.

The man nodded, then left.

Virgil's reproach had given way to his sleepiness, and he was dozing again.

And now we wait, Rose thought. *We wait to see if he survives this.*

CHAPTER 6
Handle

The crickets did not agree with Virgil. Fortunately, it turned out that dragons could vomit.

Unfortunately, the mess turned out to be so acidic that it was dangerous to handle without thick gloves. For some inscrutable reason, Henry had attempted to clean it with only a small cloth, and the skin on his palms was now red and rashy, despite his having yelped and run to the sink to run his hands under the faucet for several minutes.

This is not a good beginning, Rose thought. *I hope his feces will not be as toxic.*

They had not yet had occasion to find out, and insightful as it would no doubt be about *Deinonychus* digestive processes, Rose was not looking forward to the necessities inherent in that particular discovery. After all, she and Henry would not be the ones collecting samples and running tests on them. They would be the ones cleaning the baby.

They skipped the rat altogether, and for Virgil's second meal, they tried well-cooked and finely chopped-up chicken.

"If dragons are related to birds, that's probably closer to the kind of food his parents would have brought home," Mr. Teedle explained to everyone in the room.

Rose concurred.

To her intense relief, the chicken seemed to agree rather better with Virgil, even though he still complained about a tummyache afterwards. To Henry's obvious intense relief, the dragon did not vomit again.

Less than an hour later, the man who had been sent out returned, having visited a butcher's shop. He also carried a rather ugly, worn carpet bag, which he dropped on the floor beside Rose.

She looked at him questioningly.

"I raided my wife's closet," he said. "I presumed you wouldn't want to be wearing that dress for the rest of the day."

"Oh, thank you," Rose said, touched by his thoughtfulness. "Where is the best place for me to change?"

"There is a restroom down the hall," he said, pointing.

"Thank you," she said, picking up the carpet bag. Then she paused, remembering a complication. She hated to mention it in present company, but there were very few other options. "I'm afraid I can't undo all of the buttons on the back on my own. This dress wasn't designed for practicality."

Most of the men in the room looked hideously embarrassed. Henry held up his red, rashy hands, grimacing.

"I'll help," Mr. Teedle said briskly. "You're nearly my daughter's age. Turn around and tell me which ones you can't reach by yourself."

It was with relief that Rose was finally able to shuck the wedding dress off in the restroom several minutes later. She sorted through the carpet bag and found that Professor Anton's wife was, as she might have suspected if she'd thought about it, several sizes larger than she was. The woman was presumably her mother's age, and he had mentioned that they had four children.

Still, she was able to make do, though the brown house dress he had selected for her was quite unflattering, and hung off her arms like a dangling sack.

Never mind, Rose told herself. *Nobody here will mind if your appearance is less than presentable.*

She sighed as she tucked the wedding dress away into the carpet bag, folding it carefully, though the yards of train did not fit and had to be piled over the top between the handles. It was quite a large carpet bag, but this was not a small dress.

The thought of going back to that laboratory, and facing the stress and newness and anxiety, was difficult to persuade herself to do. But she took a long breath, in and out, and then set forth back down the hallway.

"Thank goodness," Henry said as she walked in the door. "Virgil's awake. He wants you to feed him."

Rose breathed in deeply again, and then moved to the spot on the floor where the slime from the egg had still not been cleaned up. The thin layer coating Virgil had dried into a thin, flaky crustiness all over his scales.

We need to give him a bath, Rose thought. *Can we do that safely? Do dragons bathe?*

"Hello, Virgil," she said. She reached out hesitantly, then stroked the nubs at the top of his head where horns would grow in. It was an affectionate gesture she was fairly certain she'd seen in one of his parents' memories. "Do you want to eat the same thing your father gave you before?"

Virgil wanted to have food. Virgil wanted her to feed him by mouth.

"I know you do," Rose said. "But you'll be eating out of our hands, just as before."

Virgil was sullen. Virgil was pouting.

The querulous emotion that she associated with a toddler sticking out their lower lip pushed into Rose's mind. It was all she could do to keep from laughing at the incongruity. The little dragon showed no facial expressions, nor did he have lips, but apparently some things transcended biology.

"We're going to try something different this time," Rose said. "We're going to add some stomach juices, to see if that helps you digest better."

Virgil didn't understand what that meant. Virgil wanted her to feed him by mouth.

"I know," Rose said, "but we're doing what we can do."

Virgil struggled and griped, but at last accepted the chicken with ill grace. He nearly choked at one point, and she had a brief second of panic. Then he managed to swallow, and he let out a small moan of protest before nibbling another bite out of the tiny bits of chicken in her hands.

"We need to add more water," Henry said from behind her. "If he almost choked, that means it was too dry to swallow."

"We can add a little next time," Mr. Teedle said, "but so far he hasn't complained about being thirsty, and we don't want to overdo it. Too much water can be as bad as too little."

"He may not be able to tell the difference between thirst and hunger yet," Henry challenged.

"True." Mr. Teedle looked troubled.

Virgil's eyelids drooped, and he stopped eating. He curled his tail around his body and nuzzled his head on top of it. In a moment, he was still, except for breathing.

Tentatively, Rose reached out and ran her finger along his back, hoping that it wouldn't bother him while he was sleeping. He didn't stir or even seem to notice, so she kept doing it.

The texture of his scales was slick yet soft, like snake skin. But unlike snake skin, the dragon scales seemed firmly in place, so there was no danger in rubbing against the grain, no matter what direction her finger moved in. She wondered how many dragon species had had scales like this, or if it had been a unique feature of *Deinonychus*.

She reached a part where the sticky, crusty egg slime was particularly thick, which reminded her of something she had been thinking about earlier.

"Can someone bring me a wet cloth?" Rose asked. "I'm going to clean him off."

Henry did so, and she carefully wiped the dragon's scales clean, at first very gently, and then harder and more firmly as she reached the places that held thicker layers of dried crustiness. It didn't appear to hurt Virgil; he continued to sleep soundly.

"He doesn't seem to be delicate," Henry said. "That's one thing we can be grateful for."

"But we should treat him very carefully, anyway," Rose said. "There might be areas that are unexpectedly vulnerable, like the soft spots on the heads of human babies."

Henry nodded, looking nervous.

Two hours later, they had the opportunity to deliver some insightful samples about *Deinonychus* digestive processes to an eager zoologist and two hovering biology professors. They also had the less-than-delightful opportunity to clean up the rest.

"He is going to be wearing diapers," Henry said.

Chapter 7
Haggard

After thirty-six hours, they had fallen into an exhausting rhythm. Every twenty minutes, Virgil woke up wanting to eat. He nibbled a few bites, complained again about how it wasn't the food he wanted, and then curled his tail around himself to go back to sleep.

The men left after just a few hours, Mr. Teedle promising to return in the morning. It was only after they'd left that Rose realized she hadn't eaten anything since breakfast. She nibbled a few scorched bites of the chicken, too dry and charred to offer to the infant, and offered some to Henry, too. They munched quietly until Virgil woke up again.

There seemed to be no question about going to their new apartment tonight. Trying to contact their families wasn't mentioned, either.

As night drew near, Rose yawned. She usually kept herself on a strict schedule, and her body was informing her that it was bedtime. The day had been emotionally wearying, which didn't help matters. She still felt inadequate, though Virgil's complaints had grown less vehement, and he seemed reasonably healthy.

Henry noticed her yawn. "I'll feed him for the next four hours. I'm used to staying up late to finish homework at the last minute. You go get some sleep."

Rose nodded, grateful. She picked up the carpet bag and moved to the furthest corner from the egg, where Virgil's telepathic cries would not awaken her. She settled down on the hard floor, using the bulging carpet bag as a pillow and the dress's train as a makeshift blanket across her feet.

All too soon, Henry awakened her.

"It's your turn," he said. His eyes were bloodshot, and he rubbed his neck as if it was sore.

Rose nodded, reluctantly, and stood up. She walked over to the side of the room with the egg, and found that there was no more food prepared. She sighed and started shredding chicken into the smallest pieces she could manage.

Glancing back, she saw that Henry was using the carpet bag and the dress much as she had. She tried not to be annoyed by his use of the wedding dress. It was one thing when she did it, but . . .

There are more important things to worry about right now, Rose told herself firmly.

The next few hours were agonizing. It was all she could do to stay awake while feeding Virgil. She started to doze in small spurts in between his awakenings. After four hours, she stumbled over to wake Henry, but he kept on sleeping soundly. In furious misery, she stormed back to her duty.

After seven full hours, Henry finally yawned and sat up. He glanced at his watch blearily. "You should've woken me up three hours ago," he mumbled.

"I tried," Rose snapped. "You kept sleeping."

"Oh. I'm a sound sleeper. Sorry. I've missed some morning classes that way. Just pour cold water over me or something."

"Don't tell me that," Rose said irritably. "I actually will."

"Feel free," Henry shrugged. "My father used to do that to wake me up for school. One of my roommates put ice in bed with me once when he knew I had to get up for a test."

Rose was beginning to infer a major disadvantage to living with Henry.

The tiny dragon stirred. Virgil was hungry! Virgil wanted food!

Chapter 7: Haggard

Rose groaned audibly.

"Is that him again?" Henry asked, pushing the dress's train off his legs. "I'll take care of it. You go back to sleep."

Rose should have been grateful, but she just felt grumpy. She stormed back to the corner, relieved when she passed beyond the range of Virgil's complaints. As soon as her head hit the carpet bag, she fell back asleep.

An hour later, the door squeaked open, which woke her up again. Mr. Teedle stood there, putting away his key.

"How are you doing?" he asked. "It occurred to me you probably haven't had anything to eat. I brought breakfast."

Rose peered around to the side, and saw that he was holding a basket of muffins. Her mouth watered, and she stumbled up to her feet.

"Thanks," Henry said, walking over to help himself. "We ate some of the burnt parts of the chicken, but that was it."

Rose took two muffins to assuage the hollow feeling in her stomach. She polished them off rapidly.

"How's he doing?" Mr. Teedle asked, nodding towards the sleeping dragon.

"Fine," Henry said, "I think."

Rose helped herself to another muffin. There were apple chunks in it which had not been cooked sufficiently, so they were rather chewy instead of soft, but that didn't matter. She chewed and swallowed rapidly.

Mr. Teedle hesitated. "You know," he said, "the offer still stands. The Central Park Zoo would be happy to take care of him. It would be close to the museum, and within walking distance of your home, so you could visit him frequently, just as you have here —"

"No," Henry said shortly.

"He won't take food from anyone but us," Rose reminded him.

"True," Mr. Teedle said, "but there's no reason to assume he couldn't be trained —"

"No!" Henry said vehemently. "I will not relinquish his care to strangers! He is *ours* to take care of!"

Mr. Teedle looked like he would very much like to disagree.

"Mr. Teedle," Rose said quietly, "we appreciate all you have done for us, and we'll appreciate help from whoever could do it. But Henry does not think it would be best for Virgil to be separated from us."

She didn't add that she would personally have loved to take him and the zoo up on that offer. She was tired and haggard, and did not know how they were going to manage their classes tomorrow morning. It was just as well Virgil had hatched on a Saturday.

But Henry's feelings were important, and he wasn't wrong about it. If they allowed Virgil to be taken in by strangers now, they would never truly be allowed to raise him. There were too many other people who'd consider themselves more qualified, too many other people who would have high motivations to wean him away from the parents he had chosen. Too many other people who would be more interested in his development as a research subject than as a child.

And that was not what Virgil needed.

Henry looked down at the rumpled grey suit he had worn to the wedding. He had long since removed the bow tie, and the front of the ruffled shirt was stained.

"I would like a change of clothing," he said wryly.

"As would I," Rose added. "Something from my own wardrobe, if possible."

"I can fetch clothes for you if you give me the key to your apartment," Mr. Teedle said.

Henry nodded and fumbled through his pockets. He pulled out a key and handed it over.

Rose realized with a start that she still did not have her own. She had moved most of her things to the apartment, but it had always been when Henry was home, and always when her mother or one of her roommates had been beside her, helping carry bags and acting as chaperone. Now that place would be her home, and she did not have a key.

She wondered what else they'd find they had forgotten.

"I'll fetch you something appropriate for photographs," Mr. Teedle promised. "Have you any preferences?"

"Something clean," Henry said.

"My crimson dress with the high collar and the long sleeves," Rose said. "Also fresh stockings. And my black shoes."

She was still wearing the white high heels that had been made for her mother's dress, and white was inappropriate to wear outside of weddings after Labor Day.

"Understood," Mr. Teedle said. "Would you like anything else to eat for lunch?"

"Yes," Henry said. "I want eggs. Hard-boiled eggs."

"Eggs might be a good idea," Mr. Teedle said thoughtfully. "There's every chance that he might respond well to them, too." He nodded at the dragon. "We can try to add some to his diet tomorrow."

Rose looked over at Virgil, who was still sleeping. The tip of his tail was tucked underneath him, and the large, curved claw on each of his back toes was resting against the floor.

"When can we take him home?" she wondered.

"Tomorrow morning," Mr. Teedle said. "Or tonight, if you can sneak him across the city and up to your apartment without anyone seeing. We don't want rumors spreading before the papers come out, but if you can manage that, it might be better."

And when can we tell our families? Rose wondered.

If they failed to tell their families personally, it would likely cause hurt feelings. If they spoke too soon, it would risk rumors spreading early.

"Do me a favor," Henry spoke up. "Call my family and tell them to watch for the paper tomorrow. Then they'll know why I had to leave the wedding early."

Or that's another way to handle it, Rose thought.

"Do the same for mine," she said.

Even though she suspected her mother would not be pleased at such a third-hand relaying of information.

Chapter 8
Haze

Voices were speaking on the other side of the door. Rose heard them through her tired midafternoon haze. She wished she had been able to snatch more than six hours of sleep; she did not feel she was operating at peak efficiency.

The doorknob rattled as it was unlocked, and Mr. Teedle appeared, as well as both of the paleontologists and three of the professors who had been here yesterday. Following after them were two men that Rose didn't recognize. The journalist and the photographer, presumably.

She rose. "Good afternoon, gentlemen." She had taken a seat to alleviate the ache in her feet, but she had every desire to make a good impression on them. "I'm Rose Palmer. This is Henry Wainscott."

"Mr. and Mrs. Wainscott," Henry said, walking forward to shake the strangers' hands. "You must forgive her for forgetting. We were only married yesterday."

Allow me to speak for myself! Rose thought with irritation. But it was true she had forgotten.

"Where is this thing you mentioned?" one of the men asked, craning his neck. "The dragon?"

"This way," Mr. Teedle said, guiding them around a table.

Virgil was lying on the floor, fast asleep. His snout wiggled as if he was dreaming about eating, and his tail twitched.

The two new men stared at the dragon. One of them opened the large, boxy camera he held, his hands trembling.

"This is a hoax, right?" the other man asked skeptically.

Mr. Teedle drew himself up to his full height, which was not very tall. "Young man," he said stiffly, "I am the curator of the Dragon Collection of the American Museum of Natural History. I do not perpetuate hoaxes. This is a real, live, bona fide *Deinonychus antirrhopus* dragon, hatched from an egg that we had in our possession. We do not understand the mechanism by which this egg was still alive after millions of years — it defies our current comprehension. But alive it most assuredly is."

The cameraman pressed the bulb to take his first picture. He looked very excited.

Virgil stirred and opened his eyes. He stared up at the strange men all around him, looking confused.

He wanted food. Where were his parents? He wanted food again. He was hungry. Who were all these strange minds around him?

The journalist man jumped back. "It talks!" he shouted.

"'It' is a he," Henry said waspishly. "And he's a person, just like we are. Don't you know anything about *Deinonychus* dragons?"

Do YOU know anything about Deinonychus *dragons?* Rose wanted to challenge him. As far as she was aware, Henry had had no clue that there were theories the species had been intelligent, until Virgil had awoken.

The little dragon's wings flapped slightly. His curved back claws scraped the floor.

Virgil was hungry! Virgil was getting very upset!

"Sorry, sorry," Henry said quickly, kneeling down with the bowl. "Here. Have some food."

Virgil poked his snout in Henry's hands and took a few small bites. Then he pulled back warily and eyed the camera, which was being readied to take a second picture. The cameraman scrambled to take it while the dragon was facing him.

Virgil didn't understand why the stranger was staring at him. Virgil didn't know what the box was. Why did the stranger think it was looking at him? The box was scary. It didn't have a mind.

"It's all right, it's all right," Henry soothed. "It's a camera. It's like a rock. It's not supposed to have a mind."

Virgil didn't like that the stranger thought it was looking at him. Virgil didn't like the stranger. Virgil wanted him to go away.

"Errr . . ." Henry said awkwardly, looking up. "Sorry, but . . . would you mind . . .?"

The cameraman was already moving backwards, an abashed look on his face.

"This is incredible," the journalist said. His eyebrows furrowed. "In the sense that I don't believe it. How do you make it do that?"

"I don't 'make' it do anything," Mr. Teedle said impatiently. "It is a living creature, which communicates what it thinks when it wishes."

"And 'it' is *he*," Henry added sharply. "He's a child, not a creature, and my wife and I have adopted him."

The journalist seemed very interested in this angle of the story. He began asking Henry questions and completely ignoring Rose. This irked her, so she moved over to where Henry was sitting and began to answer some of the questions herself.

"Yes, he could communicate while still in the egg," she broke in, as the journalist asked a question which she was perfectly qualified to answer. "As you can tell, his method of speaking is telepathic. That is fortunate, because it is doubtful that he could pronounce most of the sounds humans use to speak."

"'Couldn't pronounce sounds humans use to speak,'" the journalist murmured, scribbling that down in his notepad. He looked back up at Henry. "And what else can you tell me about the creature?"

Henry's eyebrows furrowed. "Well, for one thing, he's not a creature. He's a person. *Deinonychus* dragons are as intelligent as humans."

"'Very intelligent animal,'" the journalist murmured, scribbling in his notepad. "Very good, very good. What else can you tell me?"

Chapter 8: Haze

Henry looked like he wanted to hit the man.

Assuming that would not be a wise idea, Rose said quickly, "Mr. Wainscott is a student at City College. He's studying biology. I am a student at Hunter College, studying paleontology."

"'Biology and paleontology,'" the journalist murmured, scribbling. "What's paleontology again?"

"The study of fossilized animals and plants," Rose said.

"The study of dragons," Henry said at the same time.

"Ah." The journalist's confused expression cleared. "That must come in handy here." He indicated Virgil, who had finished eating and settled back to sleep with his tail curled around his feet.

"Yes," Henry said.

"Paleontologists don't just study dragons," Rose said. "They also study plants, wyverns, prehistoric mammals —"

The journalist did not write any of this down.

Soon enough, the man moved on to interview Mr. Teedle and the other experts, and the photographer crept closer.

"Do you think it would allow me to take pictures again?" he asked hopefully.

"*He*," Henry said. "And I imagine he won't notice. Please do."

The man looked relieved, and set his camera up again. He took a dozen pictures of Virgil from different angles, and then took several with the three of them together.

After that, Virgil woke up again, and this time Rose fed him. The journalist drew Henry aside to ask him more questions.

Does that man think I am not capable of speaking, or something? Rose thought with irritation.

Virgil's snout moved through her hands, licking up tiny pieces of chicken that had been moistened with water. His tongue was surprisingly dry. She wondered if that was normal, or if it was because he wasn't getting enough to drink.

Virgil raised his head up from her hands. His eyes blinked blearily, and one of his front claws scratched the floor beneath him. He looked sleepy, but curious.

His mother was annoyed. Why was his mother annoyed?

"Many reasons," Rose said, "but none have to do with you."

Virgil was sleepy. Virgil was going to take a nap.

"Please do," Rose said.

When the journalist and photographer finally left, it was quite a relief.

In the morning, Rose and Henry and an escort of three professors tucked Virgil into a large picnic basket and walked across campus to their new apartment. They had to stop twice for Henry to feed him, which he did by putting his hand into the picnic basket to avoid the swarm of onlookers that would no doubt gather if the dragon emerged. The professors left, and Henry slumped onto the couch, holding his eyes.

"I just want to sleep," he mumbled. "I wonder how many days I can skip class before it affects my GPA . . ."

"I'll be going to class," Rose said.

Henry took his hand off his eyes. "When? Obviously not today."

"Of course today. It's Monday."

Henry gave her an incredulous look. "You want to go *today?*"

"Yes. I have class today. School matters to me. I've told you that before."

"Our son *just hatched,*" Henry said. "Take a few days off."

"I will be leaving in an hour, and I'll be back at four pm," Rose said. "If you prefer, I will take Virgil with me."

"You're not going to take him away from me!" Henry exploded. "And you're not going to leave me alone for eight hours, either!"

"I don't . . . skip . . . class," Rose said coldly. "What did you think was going to happen? Did you think I was going to drop out? Is that why you got an apartment that is so near to your college and so far from mine?"

Henry appeared to be struggling with rage. "All right," he said. "Then go. Go to class!"

"I don't have to leave for another hour —" Rose began.

"Just go!" Henry shouted.

So she left.

Chapter 9
Her

It was very difficult to concentrate in her current state of exhaustion, so she took copious notes and hoped that those would compensate for her damaged attention.

After class, she started to walk back to her new apartment, and then veered off to the left through Central Park instead. She had no desire to go home right now, not after the altercation with Henry.

If she was honest with herself, she had no desire to see Virgil right now, either. The child had drained her to her last shreds of patience, and she felt like she had no more to give.

So she walked to the American Museum of Natural History, more out of habit than anything. She walked through the Hall of Ornithischian Dragons, where she had not been in weeks, admiring the *Stegosaurus* on display with its wings outstretched and the *Corythosaurus* behind glass with its wings folded.

When she reached the end, she hesitated. Hadn't she had enough of carnivorous dragons over the last few days? But it felt disloyal to not walk through the Hall of Saurischian Dragons while she was here. So she walked briskly through, intending to finish and go back home as swiftly as possible.

The *Deinonychus* eggs exhibit was the same as always, except that there were far more people surrounding it than usual.

Of course, Rose thought. *Because the newspaper will have come out by now. I really ought to look at it when I have the chance.*

She started to walk by the crowd, but then a familiar sensation hit her. The brush of a dragon's mind.

Hello! Her name was Violet! Her new father had named her! Had they met her new father yet?

Rose stopped abruptly. Her pulse quickened. Another dragon had woken up. Another dragon had woken up —

— *now,* of all times?

She shoved through the crowd, making liberal use of elbows, to the annoyance and dirty looks of those she pushed through. Rose paid that no heed. Near the front of the crowd, standing close to the display, was a filthy man with unkempt hair. He looked and smelled like a hobo.

No, Rose thought. *Surely not him.*

Violet hadn't wanted to wake up. Violet had been very sad. Violet's parents had died, along with everyone else she had known.

Rose gasped as a horrifying memory washed over her mind.

There had been a giant shaking feeling. Then all the minds around her screaming, and then silence. She screamed herself, as far as she could possibly reach, and yet nobody came to save her. She was going to die.

Some adults found her. She was carried to the orphan cave. There were hundreds of other minds there, minds like hers, minds that were young, minds that were still eggs. They were all screaming for their parents. Everyone was dead. Everyone was dead. Everyone was dead. There were hundreds of them. There were thousands. More kept coming.

There were very few adults left. All they did was bring more eggs. They didn't come to adopt any of them.

That wasn't right! That was wrong!

She seized on two of the adults when they came near her, and they said no. They were very, very sad. They said the world was wrong. They said there was no food now. They said they would come back when the world got better. They said all they could do now was save any eggs they could find.

She didn't understand. She needed parents!

She needed to not hatch right now, they said. She needed to hibernate. The babies who were hatching were dying. The eggs could only live as long as they stayed eggs, as long as they did not hatch, as long as they did not leave.

She screamed and screamed, but no one answered her. There were fewer and fewer adults. Soon, there were no adult minds at all. Only the other eggs. Only the eggs all crying.

The other eggs all started to fall asleep. She struggled to stay awake. She wanted parents. She wanted to hatch now. She wanted parents. Where were the parents?

At last, the emptiness overwhelmed her, and she too fell asleep.

Rose came back to herself. She burst out sobbing, as did others around her. The loneliness had been so absolute, the dragon's memory so desolate.

Was she alive for the extinction event? Rose thought. She tried to clean her face with her gloved hands, but more tears kept on coming. *Is that what that was? Is that what she experienced?*

Violet's father had been through awful things, too. She would show them.

The crowd burst outward, as if everyone in it was desperate to escape. For those in the front, including Rose, there was no time to get out of range.

Horrible visions exploded through her mind. There were diseases and gunshots and screaming and dying. All of his friends were killed in one day. It was so senseless, so stupid. It was the apocalypse.

Rose came back to herself, too stunned to even cry. She'd never seen anything like that. She hoped she never would again.

"That's enough of that, Violet," the hobo growled. "My memories are my own."

Rose stood where she was, too devastated to move. She had heard rumors about the Great War in Europe, had even known two neighbors' sons who had been drafted and died out there. But she had never dreamed that she would be forced to experience any of it.

Most of the other onlookers were fleeing. One mother was trying to comfort several sobbing children. One man looked like he was going to be sick.

Violet didn't understand why all the minds were leaving. Violet was sad. What had she done to make them so unhappy?

Rose breathed in and out, deeply. This wasn't what she had intended when she'd asked the other dragons to hatch. She turned to walk away.

Oh! Violet remembered her! This was the adult who had told her to hatch! This was the grown-up who had said it was time to choose parents! That was why Violet had woken up! She was so happy!

Rose turned around slowly. The filthy man was staring at her.

"You were in the paper, weren't you?" he said slowly. "You and that man. The ones with the dragon."

There seemed no point in denying it. "Yes," Rose admitted.

The man walked over and clapped his hand on her shoulder. It was all she could do to keep from flinching. "Thank you for doing that article," he said. "Gave me the gumption to come here and talk to 'em. And now I've got Violet. Ain't she a gem?"

This close, his breath reeked.

Are you aware that alcohol is illegal? Rose thought. *And you can't possibly be married. What will Violet do for a mother?*

Oh, Violet didn't need a mother! Violet was perfectly fine with just her father! Violet was so happy she had found someone who understood what she had gone through!

"Yes, you *do* need a mother!" Rose snapped out loud. "Do you have any idea how much work it takes to keep a baby dragon alive? I do! One person cannot possibly do it alone! It's not physically possible!"

The filthy man withdrew his hand, looking hurt and confused.

Violet didn't like her anymore! She didn't like Violet's father! Violet was going to take a nap.

The hobo gave Rose and angry, suspicious look. "What did she mean, you don't like me?"

Rose cringed. It was embarrassing to have been caught out.

"It's not that I don't like you," she said hastily. "It's just that . . . after all we've been through to keep Virgil alive these past few days, I don't see how one parent can do it alone. I simply don't."

"Oh." The man's expression cleared. "That's simple enough. The museum director came to talk to me this morning, after Violet first woke up. Nice man. He's arranged for her to be transferred to Central Park Zoo, where they'll pay for the food and take good care of her. Good for everyone, eh?"

Rose stared at him. She knew all the practical reasons why the zoo would work, but faced with a parent who had actually chosen that path, she was speechless.

"Name's Harrison," the man said, holding out his hand. "Pleased to meet you."

"Pleased to meet you," Rose murmured, shaking his hand gingerly. She was grateful to be wearing gloves, and hoping to wash them as soon as she arrived back home.

Home. Where Henry and Virgil were waiting.

"I must go," Rose said quickly, extricating herself. "My husband and son are expecting me. I didn't mean to stay here so long."

Husband and son. The words sounded strange as she spoke them, even as she knew they were true. Her life had changed so drastically overnight, it still astonished her.

"Go on, then," the man said cheerfully. "Maybe we can have our babies play together later. Eh?"

Maybe if you bathe yourself and don't drink your entire breakfast at a speakeasy! Rose thought.

"Perhaps," she said politely.

As she walked rapidly home, attempting to make up for lost time despite her exhaustion, her mind kept spinning around the filthy man and the new dragon. He seemed so clearly unsuitable to be a parent, and yet he had been chosen. Chosen and loved, despite all his obvious deficiencies.

Perhaps, Rose thought, *perhaps I am not so inadequate to the task as I have worried.*

Chapter 10
Henry

Henry was asleep on the couch when she walked in. His hand was dangled on the floor next to Virgil's head, and it was filled with a large clump of watery, shredded chicken. Some had dripped on the floor and scattered along the carpet.

That seems a fairly good solution, Rose thought, setting aside the shoulder bag she had used to carry her notes and writing implements. *Has Virgil been helping himself while Henry sleeps?*

As if on cue, the little dragon stirred. His front claws dug into the carpet, and he raised his head, his eyes wide open.

Virgil wanted food now. Virgil wanted his father to wake up so that he could eat. Virgil wanted his father to wake up so that he could eat. Virgil wanted his father to wake up so that he could eat. Virgil wanted his father to wake up so that he could eat.

Henry groaned and stirred. He sat up, his eyes still shut, and held out his hand. Their son's scaly head darted forward.

Apparently he has not been able to sleep while Virgil helped himself, Rose thought. *A pity.*

The hatchling's head jerked away from the food.

Virgil's mother was home! He hadn't noticed! Could she feed him, too?

"Oh, are you home?" Henry murmured. His eyes cracked open. "Good. Does that mean I can sleep?"

"Go ahead," Rose said, though her eyes ached and her legs felt leaden. "I'll feed him for awhile. Is there anything prepared?"

"Bowl in the kitchen," Henry muttered, staggering to his feet. "Your parents called. Read the newspaper."

"What did they say?" Rose asked, her heart hammering.

Virgil was still hungry! The food was gone! Virgil wanted his food! Virgil's mother needed to give him food!

Henry rubbed his eyes, then stopped and stared down at the hand covered in chicken, which he had just smeared all over his face and dropped down the front of his shirt. He muttered something unintelligible that was likely profane.

"Language," Rose said, just in case.

Henry looked grumpy. "Your mother said they wanted to meet the dragon. Your father said, 'Is this real?' One of your sisters, I'm not sure which, said, 'Trust Rose to find a live dragon!' Then the other said, 'Can we get one?' —"

"He's not a pet," Rose said peevishly.

"I'm aware," Henry began.

Virgil was very, very, very hungry! Virgil's parents needed to feed him! He was going to scream!

Rose yanked off her gloves and lunged for the chicken still on Henry's hand. She got her hand down to the floor just as the earsplitting screech began. She waved her hand up and down frantically until the little dragon noticed.

Virgil thought that was better. Virgil was going to eat now.

A rough, dry tongue began to gather up bits of watery chicken from her hand, the little dragon emanating indignation.

"What else did they say?" Rose asked.

"Not much," Henry said, shrugging. "I told them you went to class. Your mother didn't believe it at first. Your sisters thought it was hilarious. Your father said, 'Why am I not surprised?'"

Rose took a little pride in that.

"Speaking of which," Henry said, "we need to come up with something to make our schedules compatible. We really do."

Rose swallowed. She hadn't forgotten how angry Henry had been this morning, and she supposed he hadn't, either.

"I'm sorry," she said. "I should have thought to mention it before, but with all that happened so quickly —"

"No," Henry said, his jaw twitching. "Don't apologize. I'll just get mad all over again. I'm tired and I'm not thinking straight. Just . . . we need to think of something. That's all. I'm not going to quit school, either. You understand?"

Rose nodded vehemently. She would never want a husband who hadn't finished his education.

"I only have one class on Tuesdays and Thursdays," she said. "It's still early in the semester. I imagine I can drop it, or attempt to find another time it's held between the classes I have on the other three days."

"That's a start," Henry said. He yawned widely. "Got to sleep now. Good night."

"Good night," Rose said, though it was midafternoon.

He staggered off to the bedroom, leaving her alone with the dragon. Their son, the dragon.

"Hey, Virgil?" Rose said quietly. "Thank you for choosing us."

A scaly face with yellow eyes looked up at her.

Virgil was glad he'd chosen them, too. Even though they looked strange. And they didn't feed him real food.

Rose hesitated, because she wasn't prone to bursts of affection, and then leaned forward and kissed the top of the tiny dragon's head.

Virgil paused in his eating. Why had his mother done that? There was no food on his head.

"It's a way that humans show affection," Rose said. "I'm getting used to you."

That was good. Virgil was used to her, too. Where was more food? He had finished. Where was more food?

Rose got up and went to the kitchen, where she found the bowl Henry had mentioned. She scooped some of the contents into her hand and walked back to the living room, where the dragon was digging into the carpet with his curved back claws.

Chapter 10: Henry

"You're destroying the carpet," Rose said. "Please stop."

Virgil was hungry. Virgil didn't know what a carpet was. Where was Virgil's food?

She bent down and gave it to him. While the dragon was eating, she checked the thick cloth they had wrapped around his nether regions. It was, unfortunately, sopping wet.

Once he was asleep, she got up and walked to the kitchen, where she found a replacement small towel in a bottom drawer. Then she clusmily undid the safety pins and wrapped the new towel around his bottom and the top part of his tail. She carefully fastened the safety pins back again.

Rose breathed out a sigh of relief.

I can do this.

She stood up and took the disgusting, soaked towel to the kitchen, where she proceeded to wash it with soap in the sink. Then she wrung it out and hung it to dry over the top of a lower cabinet door.

She walked back to the living room, where Virgil lay curled up with his tail around him. His snout wriggled as his curved back claws attacked the carpet.

I can do this, Rose thought.

She sat down, intending to start on her homework, and then Virgil raised his head and looked at her.

He was hungry. Where was his food? He was hungry.

I hope I can do this, Rose thought with a sigh, returning to the kitchen to get him more chicken.

$\mathscr{C}$HAPTER 11
Hello

"L ook at that little tail!" Rose's mother exclaimed. "It's so long and thin and scaly! Does he use it for balance? It seems to be so flexible. Oh, that dragon is so sweet!"

Virgil wriggled and squirmed in a circle, trying to catch sight of it. His legs couldn't support his weight, so all he could do was scoot around and leave claw marks in the carpet.

Why was this person so excited about his tail? What was so special about his tail? He wanted to see.

Rose's father let out a snort that sounded like an attempt to disguise laughter.

"Why does he have those things?" Louise demanded, pointing at the long, curved claw that defied the length of all the others on each of his back feet. "You should trim them. They look dangerous."

"I'm not going to trim them; that's normal for his species," Rose said. "*Deinonychus* means 'terrible claw.' That's where the name came from."

"I want a pet dragon," Sara sighed wistfully.

"He's *not a pet*," Henry growled.

"But there were lots of other dragon species, too, right?" Louise asked excitedly. "What if somebody found live eggs from one of them? Then there could be such a thing as a dragon pet!"

Chapter 11: Hello

Rose was highly disturbed at the idea. It was one thing to find that one species had survived, especially an intelligent one. But a dozen other dragon species . . .? The ecological niches those species had filled were now taken, and the world did not need invasive species to threaten the ones that were now living.

Although perhaps, Rose thought, a little shaken as she followed her own line of reasoning, *perhaps humans have filled the role that* Deinonychus *once held. Perhaps, by encouraging them to live and grow and procreate and eventually restore the species, we may be encouraging our own extinction?*

The thought was chilling. She shivered.

Please hatch, she had asked the other eggs, and one of them had awoken. Surely the others would soon be forthcoming. What if New York City, in a few generations, would be overrun by terrible claws who wished to wipe out humanity?

She stepped on the thought firmly. So there was danger. What of it? There was hope, as well. If it came down to it, their species could learn to coexist. Nature was vicious and cruel, but people need not be.

For now, and for the future, she would focus on hope. Hope for her son's future. Hope for the future of *Deinonychus.*

"You know, when my wife told me she thought there might be a child in the picture," Rose's father broke in, "this wasn't exactly what I envisioned."

Rose's mother gave him a furious look. It was clear that this had not been a conversation she had wished repeated.

I knew it, Rose thought, her fists tightening. *I knew that was what our relations had to be thinking. I certainly hope we can disabuse them of that notion swiftly. Without, of course, mentioning the subject directly.*

There were some things that one just didn't do. Unless one was Rose's father, apparently.

Henry's face turned red. It didn't look like he had considered the possibility of rumors at all. "S-sir," he sputtered, "I assure you . . ."

Rose's father watched him squirm with evident amusement.

"Is he healthy?" Rose's mother broke in, rubbing the top of the dragon's head. "Is he eating well?"

Rose smiled at the concern in her mother's voice. It seemed like her mother had accepted Virgil as family. "He seems to be all right, so far. We've added chicken fat and egg yolks to the chicken mixture, and that seems to be beneficial. He's now sleeping an hour between feedings, rather than fifteen minutes."

A trend she profoundly hoped would continue. Since tomorrow would be her first day alone with Virgil, now that she had changed her schedule, she very much wanted the time to do her homework.

Virgil's stomach hurt. Virgil was uncomfortable.

"Uh oh," Henry said, diving to the floor. "You might, uh . . . want to leave now. I expect we're going to have to clean up a mess."

Virgil's stomach hurt now!

"Understood," Rose's mother said hastily. "We'll leave you to it. Virgil, it was nice to meet you and say hello."

Virgil's stomach hurt! Hurt, hurt, hurt!

Rose's mother rushed to the door, her father following at a rapid pace. Rose's sisters hovered in the doorway curiously to watch as Henry gathered up the baby.

"Thank you for visiting," Rose hinted strongly. "It's a shame you have to leave now."

"Louise! Sara!" their father barked from all the way down the hallway.

Looking reluctant, her sisters turned away.

"I want a pet *Brontosaurus*," Sara said to Louise. "They have the best wings."

"It's *Apatosaurus*," Rose shouted after them, "and no, you don't!"

Do they have any idea how large that dragon used to be? Rose thought with exasperation, locking the door firmly after her family.

She found Henry in the bathroom, where he had placed their son in the bathtub. The hatchling seemed less than thrilled about this.

Virgil was sleepy. Maybe Virgil would take a nap. He needed to get out of this box now.

"Oh, no, you don't," Henry said.

Virgil didn't like this box! It was white and cold and there was nothing to claw!

"How very unfortunate," Henry snorted.

Virgil liked that noise. He was going to snort, too. Snort, snort, snort, snort —

A roar of flame burst from his nostrils and reached the towel on the rack across from him.

Henry's mouth fell open.

Rose leapt forward, seized the towel, and dunked it in the toilet, which doused it. She pulled it out, dripping. A huge black hole was now eaten in the once-serviceable object.

Virgil's stomach felt better now.

"Well," Rose said after a moment of silence, "at least we know when *Deinonychus* dragons start breathing fire. That's been a mystery for centuries."

"This is going to be so much worse than potty training," Henry groaned.

www.ingramcontent.com/pod-product-compliance
Lightning Source LLC
Chambersburg PA
CBHW022122050726

47591CB00002B/889